First Day at
Zoo School

By Sarah Dillard

It was the first day of Zoo School.
Mrs. Wattles was ready.

Amanda
was ready.

Alfred?
He was not so sure.

As Amanda approached the school,
she realized she was missing something.

Then she saw
Alfred.

Mrs. Wattles welcomed the class.

At lunch, Alfred tried to be invisible.

But it didn't work.

Amanda knew just how she wanted to spend recess.

When it was time to go home, Amanda led the way.

The next day, all day long
Amanda and Alfred were not friends.

At lunch
Amanda and Alfred
sat by themselves.

My cookie
needs some
banana.

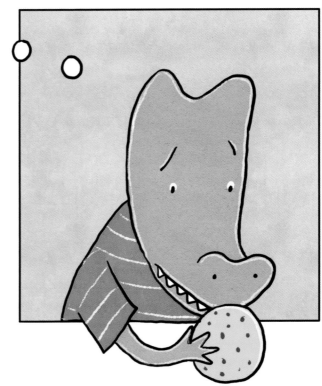

After lunch Amanda climbed a tree and hung upside down.

Finally, Alfred just couldn't stand it anymore.

If your head bursts then we can never be best friends again.

With special thanks to Maddy Eaton
—Sarah

Sleeping Bear Press™

315 E. Eisenhower Parkway, Ste. 200
Ann Arbor, MI 48108
www.sleepingbearpress.com

Printed and bound in the United States.

10 9 8 7 6 5 4 3 2

Library of Congress Cataloging-in-Publication Data

Dillard, Sarah, 1961- author, illustrator.
First day at Zoo School / by Sarah Dillard.
pages cm
Summary: "On the first day of school, vivacious Amanda the Panda meets anxious Alfred
the Alligator. But when Amanda decides that Alfred would be the perfect best friend for
her, the difference in their temperaments leads to hurt feelings"—Provided by publisher.
ISBN 978-1-58536-890-7
[1. Individuality—Fiction. 2. Friendship—Fiction. 3. Pandas—Fiction.
4. Alligators—Fiction. 5. Schools—Fiction.] I. Title.
PZ7.D57733Fir 201
[E]—dc23
2013050599